Like a

HURRICANE

...told me that at my birth... with a burning forehead... She'd never breathed... that at my birth it was hard for air to get through... difficulties... breathing difficulties.

ready to be that terrible fright again, that terrible fright again
to tell her who I am. I don't want to make her go through

I hesitate.

Like a

HURRICANE

Jonathan Bécotte

TRANSLATED BY
Jonathan Kaplansky

ORCA BOOK PUBLISHERS

Published in Canada and the United States in 2023 by Orca Book Publishers.
Originally published in French in 2020 by Les éditions Héritage inc.
under the title *Comme un ouragan*.
orcabook.com

Library and Archives Canada Cataloguing in Publication
Title: Like a hurricane / Jonathan Bécotte ; translated by Jonathan Kaplansky.
Other titles: Comme un ouragan. English
Names: Bécotte, Jonathan, 1987- author. | Kaplansky, Jonathan, 1960- translator.
Description: Translation of: Comme un ouragan.
Identifiers: Canadiana (print) 2022022286X | Canadiana (ebook) 20220222878 |
ISBN 9781459835238 (softcover) |
ISBN 9781459835245 (PDF) | ISBN 9781459835252 (EPUB)
Classification: LCC PS8603.E4235 C6613 2023 | DDC jC843/.6—dc23

Library of Congress Control Number: 2022936540

Summary: In this novel in verse for middle readers, a young teen struggles with revealing who he really is to those he loves.

Orca Book Publishers gratefully acknowledges the support for its publishing programs provided by the following agencies: the Government of Canada, the Canada Council for the Arts and the Province of British Columbia through the BC Arts Council and the Book Publishing Tax Credit.

We acknowledge the financial support of the Government of Canada through the National Translation Program for Book Publishing, an initiative of the *Roadmap for Canada's Official Languages 2013-2018: Education, Immigration, Communities*, for our translation activities.

Translated by Jonathan Kaplansky
Edited by Tanya Trafford
Cover illustration by Grandfailure/Creative Market
Author photo by Alana Riley
Translator photo by Véro Boncompagni

Printed and bound in Canada.

26 25 24 23 • 1 2 3 4

To Geneviève, my Zoé.

I would like to thank Christopher Cuellar, my partner in life, for helping me cross the bridge between the translator's words and my own.
—J.B.

Outside, the wind fades the sky, the houses.
The heart changes; suddenly it carries the city away,
behind us with the past.
—Élise Turcotte, *La terre est ici*

Throughout this story, you must never
lose sight of the wind.
—Anne Hébert, *In the Shadow of the Wind*,
tr. Sheila Fischman

My grandmother used to say
that when the wind blows the leaves around,
the weather will change.

I feel that soon
my breath will make *the trees bend.*

It's not easy to keep a secret.
I was never good at that.
Especially when it's a secret as

as the one rumbling in my stomach.

For a few months now,
my breathing has changed.

Where my voice meets my breath,
my throat seems to have shrunk.

When I exhale,
I **def**late almost entirely.

I constantly run out of air.
It's like I am racing in a marathon
but the finish line
keeps
moving.

Running after yourself leaves you breathless.

This morning my father said to me,

"You're really short of breath lately. Is everything okay?"

"Is something on your mind, my love?"
asked Mom.

It's as if they can hear
my secret reverberating.

An alarm sounding,
an ear-shattering radio signal,
as disturbing as the one that warns
people that a hurricane is brewing.

My thoughts are trembling.
The ground below is in turmoil.
I answer them very softly,
my lungs almost empty:

"No…everything's fine."

I am lying.

The ground cracks   beneath my feet.

There is a wind turbine
between my lungs.
Its blades
slice through the air as they turn.
Their sound cuts off the **words**
that I can't manage to utter.

I'm afraid that the truth,
my truth,
the one whistling in my heart,
will carry away my house and my family
all at the same time.

I don't like to disturb people.
I wasn't born to be a hurricane.
But I can no longer
hold back the winds inside,
can no longer silence what resounds
within me.

echoing
echoing
echoing
echoing
echoing
echoing
echoing

I want to
shatter
everything,
tear off
roofs,

knock down

skyscrapers,

travel through the country

destroying all that stands before me,

to **O**pen my mouth

to **tell** them.

I've always known
that I wasn't like
other kids my age.
I always felt
that I was

separate from the others.

I couldn't recognize myself
in library books.
Knights and princesses,
firemen and ballerinas.

No book ever told the story
of boys who like to pick flowers
instead of playing s/⌒γ⁰ccer.

I didn't play with miniature cars.
I watched over my cuddly toys—
I cradled them.
I invented ailments for them
so that they could spend more time
in my arms.

I didn't know the names of professional
athletes
or wrestlers or collect
their action figures.
I didn't like **fighting**
or pretending to bleed.

Instead I played school
with the younger girls in my neighborhood.
I made up lessons for them
and corrected their drawings with a red felt-tip pen.

My mother sometimes had to deal with people
and their comments about me.
They always had things to say
about how I was *behaving*
or how I was *acting*.

I pretended not to notice,
but I saw the pointed noses
and the pinched lips
when they looked at me
and leaned over to
whisper something in my mom's ear.

Once, in the park, a lady said to her:

"If your son flutters around like that,
he'll end up flying away."

You should know that when I'm really happy,
my arms start to flap
like the wings of a gull.

My best friend's father nicknamed me
the sparrow.
He said I reminded him of the main character
in his favorite book.

"Your son is really sensitive.
He cries over nothing," the teacher at daycare
once commented.

Crying has always been a part of me.

It feels good.
It's important.
It allows sadness
to leave my body.

Mom says that when you cry,
you're trying to soothe a burn,
calm pain,
cool down your machine.

In the schoolyard, a man once joked:
"He is so little, so frail.
A good gust of wind could
lift him off the ground."

I am not

STRONG,

true.

But I am

flexible.

I can
tuck my legs behind my neck.

I always wanted to do gymnastics,
or ballet, like my cousin.
But my parents enrolled me
in judo,
hockey
and baseball.

I choreograph dances
for my invisible audience,
in my room
or behind the shed.

When people speak to my mother about me,
they think they know everything about me.
She just smiles
and runs a loving hand
through my hair.

Their remarks

go a thousand feet
above her head.

"He is very emotional."

"He isn't like other boys."

"He is *soft,* too soft…"

Yet she has no idea
of the power of the tornado
inside me, contained in my heart.
There's a tsunami, a typhoon,
padlocked in my chest.

And in the middle of this whirlwind,

YOU. there is

A special friend,
my forever sidekick.
As if we had existed before
Once upon a time.

Our mothers were both pregnant at the same time.
When we were still in their wombs,
their bellies almost touching,
they said to one another,
"For sure, they'll be best friends."

And it's true—
we went through so much together.

Our first day of kindergarten.

Your first tooth falling out.

Mine.

Licorice evenings at the drive-in.

Being afraid of the monsters
that we imagined.

Our horror-movie marathons.

Our last time falling off our bikes
before removing the training wheels.

Our hikes on the grounds
of an old closed-down factory.

Our Decembers believing in Santa Claus.

Our spy missions in stairwells.

YOU

were front and center.
A full-time job,
at the center of my life.

At school
we were always in the same group,

you
and
me.

You thought it was a coincidence,
but my mother always requested it.

You made me happy.
Our friendship lasted through the years.
You were my calendar.

But lately
we hardly talk to each other.

We don't even wait for the bus on the same corner.

You became a ghost,
and I'm invisible to your eyes,
as if I've become transparent.
Like mist, a cloud.

Speaking of clouds,
for my final project in elementary school,
we have to build an object that measures
an aspect of the weather.

Mom came up with an idea I like a lot:

"Why not a weather vane?"

It's true that I know the
compass points well,
even though sometimes I get lost
on the way between school and home.

Especially
in autumn,
when
leaves
fall
and
disguise
the streets

I'm thinking of the compass rose.
Something beautiful and fragile
that blooms to show us
which way the wind blows.

My parents help me build
my weather vane.
I want it to be perfect.
I spend a lot of time on the finishing touches,
choosing the materials, the colors,
the textures, the dimensions.

For two weeks
we spend every evening
in the dust of Dad's workshop.
He works with the wood that I paint
as if it were a work of art.

But despite our efforts,
my compass rose never manages to find north.

I don't know what to think anymore or which way to turn. I am the weather vane whirling wildly around on a farmhouse roof as a storm approaches.

I feel defective,
like my science project.

With all my strength,
I hurl my weather vane,
and it shatters into pieces
against the concrete wall.

I would have liked to hurl my head there too,
to stop the ideas
that keep spinning round.

Why
isn't it working?

What isn't
working?

What's
wrong
with me?

Dad picks up the pieces of my **broken**
project.
He taps me on the shoulder.
I hold out my hands.
He places the fragments in them.

"You're going to have to make something with that,
son," he tells me.
"Come and see me when you are ready."

I wipe away a few tears.
I try to glue the bird's beak back on.
I must confide my secret to someone.
Before I lose my head,
like my weather vane.

I'll talk about it with Zoé,
my best friend.
She's like my sister.
She knows almost everything about me.

She and I

are neighbors.

Our houses are diagonally across from each other.

I can see her bedroom window

from mine.

At night, before going to sleep,
we create light shows.
We flash our bedside lamps
to wish each other good night.
We light stars for each other.

We form a trio, she, you and me.

Well, not anymore.

You cast us   aside.

What I like the most about Zoé
is her way of expressing herself.
She always speaks very loudly
and is never still.

She doesn't come over to my place that much,
because she exhausts my parents.
Like in summer, when I invite her for a swim,
we're not allowed to jump.
Mom says the pool will overflow.

In the evening, after eight o'clock,
you have to keep your voice down.
My friend only knows one volume:
at the top of her **lungs**.

I am rather shy.
She, not at all.

Zoé is my favorite tidal wave.
She's the one I want to reveal my secret to
first.

Oh shoot, I won't have time
to talk to her about it today.
I forgot—
we have gym class.
We won't be together all day.

I'll have to wait until after school.
My secret isn't the kind that
I can tell between two periods,
in a corridor filled with people.

I've always hated
PE classes.
Especially because they often separate

the girls

from the boys.

That shouldn't happen,
separating friends from friends.

For these gym sessions,
I elbow my way to stand tall.
But I often drop the ball
and miss the hoop every time.

The other boys shove me.
I'm in their way
like a weed.

"Shut up, wuss!"
big Luke shouts at me.

That word makes me think
of the fluff of a dandelion.
A useless flower

that you
pull   out
and

whose seeds

d r i f t   a p a r t

with
the

slightest
breeze.

To survive gym class
I think of the girls I'm friends with,
who are playing with ribbons
on the other side of the wall.

I'd like to be taken by the wind,
leave through the window,
come apart like a dandelion.
Join them in their gymnastics area
covered with mats.

There, when you fall, it doesn't hurt.

Sometimes I tell myself that life
is a game of basketball.
You're handed a number at birth,
as if the doctor were choosing your place,
the team on which you'll play.

I'm afraid he got it wrong,
that the team he assigned me to
is making me lose the game.

All that's because of you!

You who were always in my class.

In my life.

In my head.

In my heart.

You who are still there
but are now light-years away
from what we had,
from what we were.

Now
when I greet you with a wave of the hand,
it's as if I were a draft.

Muttering,
you barely acknowledge me.

You answer me with

disjointed to d i s t a n c e me,

words muzzled, filled with shame.

The most horrific racket
is the sound of your silence.

I remember
when I gave you

a best-friend necklace for your birthday!

I chose one with a
yin and yang pattern.

I bought it from a florist.
She placed it in a small box
lined with white foam.
A box in which a jeweler
could have placed a gold necklace.

I paid for it with money
from the tooth fairy.

It cost me my entire

smile.

I still wear my half.
I never took it off,
even though the **rusted chain** stains
my neck
and leaves marks on my pillow.

That memory of us corrodes in my dreams.

I look discreetly at your neck.
You no longer wear it.

Do you remember the hours we spent
building castles
out of sand, cards or blankets?

Do you remember when we escaped,
disappearing
to prolong our games of hide-and-seek?
How good it felt

to be hidden
from the rest
of the world?

We pretended to be adventurers.
We discovered things
that no one else knew about.

You know, you always gave me
little butterflies in my stomach.
I didn't understand the reason for that rumbling
at the time.
I thought perhaps it was a virus,
a contagious disease.

You made me dizzy,
made me airsick.
You took my serenity and sent it away in a hot-air balloon.

Today, touching the warmth
on my cheeks,
I know I'm not sick.

When I notice you out of the corner of my eye,
when you collect books from your locker,
near mine,
when you laugh with your group of friends...

Now I know it's you
who was creating the fizzing in my stomach.

Because of you, everything is confused
today.
I can no longer talk about what I am
without thinking of your face
and our memories.

You are

at the center

of everything.

But the wind has turned between us. The beating of my heart distanced you from me. You ran away from those explosions in my rib cage.

I still feel those

e**X**plo_s**i**_o**n**_s

today,
when I see Zoé waiting for me at the bus.
She winks at me;
that calms the fanfare in my chest.

On the ride home,
we've gotten into the habit of building
a makeshift shelter
with our hoodies joined
at the sleeves.
We disappear from the rest of the world.

Zoé knows I have something to tell her.
She has her *it will be okay* smile.
In our hoodie shelter,
untouched by time,
I share my secret with my best friend.

A few

minutes

go by,

our cheeks pressed together.

Then my friend kisses
my forehead.

"I always knew. I was waiting
for you to be ready to talk to me about it.
I'm so lucky
to have you in my life."

We almost miss our stop.
When we get off the bus,
we hug each other.

"I'm going to tell my parents this evening," I say.

"I'll leave my light on.
Good luck, my star. Everything will be fine."

Arriving home,
I shut myself in my room.

To
breathe,

to calm the storm
brewing inside me.

My bed

is an island where

I go to catch my breath

before diving back into my life.

I'm a rain shower.
I drench my pillow
with the emotions that I hold back all
day.
The ones I hide in the gym,
in the too-long corridors,
in the classrooms where we're placed in
alphabetical order.

I overflow
like a river when winter melts.
Yet today is different.
I'm crying, yes, but not out of sorrow.
A new,
gentler feeling
arose between my cheek and Zoé's.

My grandmother used to say
that a secret is less of a

BURDEN

to carry
when it is shared.

Zoé now has a copy of the key
to my treasure chest.
I think I'll stop by the hardware store.
There are other copies to be made.

Evening is approaching.
The sky darkens.

A storm is forecast tonight.

CRASH of thunder.

CANNON fire.

A DRAMATIC turn.

It's my bedroom door slamming—
the door I must open.

In acting class, I learned
that you always knock several times
before an actor goes onstage.
It's a ritual.
Something significant.

I'm preparing to give
the most important performance of my life:

showing the w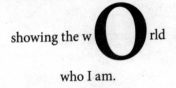rld

who I am.

Suddenly I remember
what my mother told me
a long time ago.

When she became pregnant with me,
she stopped smoking.
She told me it was easy.
You protect a baby from fire.

It's funny, because she said sometimes that,
even though she hadn't smoked
for several months,
she still felt
a burning sensation in her throat.

I think it was because of me.
I was like a fire
in her belly.
I was the one who gave her
the taste of ashes in her mouth.

A sign that she was going to give birth to
a little phoenix,
a bird rising from the ashes,
a child who'd have to be born a second time.

She also told me that at my birth
I had a high fever.
An infant with a burning forehead.

I was intubated
due to breathing difficulties.
It was hard for air to get through.
She'd never been so frightened.

Now that I'm ready to be reborn,
to tell her who I am,
I hesitate.

I don't want to cause a forest fire.
I don't want to make her go through
that terrible fright again,
the fear of losing me.

I want to be a spark in her hands.
A firefly,
light and warm.

But

my secret's
blowing

too hard

for me to

suffocate it one

more

day.

I must take the risk that sparks will fly.

Outside, lightning shatters a branch,
bringing me back to myself.
Gripping the doorknob,
I leave my room.

"Mom...Dad...
I have something
to tell you."

Walking to the living room, I pass
a portrait of my grandfather,
hanging on the wall
near my parents' bedroom.
He learned to play
the bagpipes at a young age.

"You need strong lungs to play that
instrument! You have to be able to
fill yourself with air and have enough left over to give it
all you've got," he'd told me.

My mother and my father are seated side by side
on the living room couch.

"We're listening, son."

"What do you want to tell us, sweetheart?"

I open my mouth
like a diver
coming out of water for his first breath of air.

"Mom, Dad...
I am gay."

Uttering these five words,
I feel a huge weight lifting
off my shoulders.
I feel a strong wind
leave my stomach
and fill my lungs.

Breathing,
for real,
for the first time.

That's what Grandpa meant
by "you need strong lungs,"
to be able to give it all you've got,
to open up.

By reflex
I put my hands in front of my face
to create a screen.

I'm scared to see their eyes,
like when you think you've done
something bad.

My mother stands up,
placing one hand in the middle of my back.
In a very calm voice,
like the sound of a breeze in the leaves
of a tree,
she murmurs,

"That's okay, my love.
Now breathe."

"Yes, breathe, my son," Dad echoes.

The living room fills with warmth.
It's as if they've just lit
a log fire.
We hug.

MY PARENTS,

TWO SOLID LOGS
STANDING BY EACH OTHER.

I, in the middle,
the flame
that sparkles.

We remain like that
for a while.

Without a crackle.

Without a hurricane.

"You are our child.
We love you for who you are."

"We love all of you.
Thank you for confiding in us."

That same evening,
after the storm,
we went to fly a kite,

without
fear
of
lightning.

And way up high,
fastened to the end of the string,
my heart floated among the clouds.

From now on,
I'll fly
above the comments
of the other parents,
above the insults,
above your silence.

Like the firebird,

I will shine spectacularly bright.

Now
I am

ME.

Completely me.
For real.
And I've learned to breathe again—
I've found my breath once more.

JONATHAN BÉCOTTE is the author of a number of works for young people. The French edition of *Like A Hurricane, Comme un ouragan*, was nominated for the Governor General's Literary Award in 2021, as was his earlier young adult novel in verse, *Maman veut partir* (2018). Jonathan has won the Prix Cécile-Gagnon and the Prix Alvine-Bélisle. He lives in Montreal, where he teaches elementary school.

JONATHAN KAPLANSKY received his BA from Tufts University and an MA in French language and literature at McGill University, as well as an MA in translation at the University of Ottawa. He has translated works by Annie Ernaux, Jean-Pierre Le Glaunec, Lise Tremblay, John Porter, Hélène Dorion, Hélène Rioux, Étienne Beaulieu and Simon Brault. He lives in Montreal.

ready to be that terrible fright again, that terrible fright again
to tell her who I am. I don't want to make her go through
hesitate.